GOOD D🐾G
3

Herd You Loud and Clear

by
Cam Higgins

illustrated by
Ariel Landy

LITTLE SIMON

New York London Toronto Sydney New Delhi

LITTLE SIMON
An imprint of Simon & Schuster Children's Publishing Division
1230 Avenue of the Americas, New York, New York 10020
First Little Simon hardcover edition December 2020
Copyright © 2020 by Simon & Schuster, Inc.
Also available in a Little Simon paperback edition.
All rights reserved, including the right of reproduction in whole or in part in any form. LITTLE SIMON is a registered trademark of Simon & Schuster, Inc., and associated colophon is a trademark of Simon & Schuster, Inc.
For information about special discounts for bulk purchases, please contact Simon & Schuster Special Sales at 1-866-506-1949 or business@simonandschuster.com.
The Simon & Schuster Speakers Bureau can bring authors to your live event. For more information or to book an event contact the Simon & Schuster Speakers Bureau at 1-866-248-3049 or visit our website at www.simonspeakers.com.
Designed by Leslie Mechanic
Manufactured in the United States of America 1120 MTN
10 9 8 7 6 5 4 3 2 1
Library of Congress Cataloging-in-Publication Data
Names: Higgins, Cam, author. | Landy, Ariel, illustrator.
Title: Herd you loud and clear / by Cam Higgins; illustrated by Ariel Landy.
Description: First Little Simon paperback edition. | New York: Little Simon, 2020. | Series: Good dog; #3 | Audience: Ages 5–9. | Audience: Grades K–1.
Identifiers: LCCN 2020019855 | ISBN 9781534479067 (paperback) | ISBN 9781534479074 (hardcover) | ISBN 9781534479081 (eBook)
Subjects: CYAC: Sheep dogs—Fiction. | Dogs—Fiction. | Sheep—Fiction. | Farm life—Fiction. | Friendship—Fiction.
Classification: LCC PZ7.1.H54497 Her 2020 | DDC [E]—dc23
LC record available at https://lccn.loc.gov/2020019855

CONTENTS

Puffs

How in the world do sheep stay so fluffy—no matter what they do?

Whenever I spend the day playing outside in the field, my fur gets tangled and wild. If I take a nap lying against a tree, my fur is smooshed flat and totally dirty when I wake up.

And I don't even want to tell you what happens when I roll around in the barn.

But sheep are different from dogs. No matter what they do, they are always puffy. Their wool seems to stay bouncy and cheerful like a cloud all the time.

There is just one problem. Even though they look super soft, sheep do *not* like to be used as pillows. I learned that the hard way.

There is something that sheep *do* love: playing hide-and-seek. And that  was what we were doing on a sunny afternoon.

My buddy Puffs was hiding. I was seeking.

Puffs is a very nice sheep, and he's a really good friend. But he's not the best at playing hide-and-seek.

When he's the seeker, he almost always forgets that we are playing a game. If something catches his eye, he'll wander over to check it out and forget to come find me!

And if he is the one hiding, well, let's just say he doesn't always remember how fluffy and white he is . . . and it's hard enough to find good hiding spots in an open green field.

If Puffs hides
behind a tree—I
found you!

If Puffs hides
behind a big hay
bale—I found you!

If Puffs hides
behind another
sheep—well, that's a
little bit trickier, but
still—I found you!

Today Puffs tried hiding next to the cows grazing in the field.

"Found *MOO*!" I yelled, and the cows laughed so hard, I think a little milk came out of their noses.

"Aw, that's no fair!" Puffs said. "You're too good at this game, Bo! You always find me. Hmm, are you sure you're not cheating?"

"No way!" I told Puffs. "Dogs never cheat. It's impossible. We're just not built that way."

"Then how in the world did you find me?" the young sheep asked. "This hiding spot was perfect!"

I didn't have the heart to tell him that while cows are bigger than sheep, they have spots, and they are not fluffy.

You see, cows and sheep do not look anything alike, but they don't smell alike either. I mean, they are totally different animals. So when a sheep tries to blend in with a herd of cows to fool a dog like me, it doesn't work. They stick out like, well, a woolly sheep.

"Hmm," I said, thinking, "maybe I am just a lucky hide-and-seeker."

Puffs nodded. "Yeah, that must be it. Because I know this was a really good hiding spot."

As we headed back toward the flock of sheep, Puffs listed some other games we could play.

"Have you ever played tag?" he asked me.

"Yep, that's fun," I answered.

"What about freeze tag?" he tried.

"Yep, I've played that, too," I said.

"Oh! What about sheep frog?" Puffs asked.

"Nope," I said. "Wait. Um, is that like leapfrog, where you hop over your friends?"

"Yes, but in sheep frog, you hop over sheep friends," said Puffs. "But it sounds like you've played it. Gosh, Bo. Is there *any* game you aren't good at?"

I thought for a minute, then said, "I'm sure there is, but we will have to find it later. I have a few more pup chores to do before dinner tonight. See you tomorrow?"

"Okay," said Puffs. "But I'm going to find a game that you've never ever played. I promise!"

I chuckled as he bounded over to his sheep friends. If anyone could find a game like that, it would probably be Puffs.

The Baa Baa Shop

The next morning Rufus the rooster woke everybody up with an amazingly loud cock-a-doodle-doo.

I got up right away, all ready to get my day started. My human family was a different story. It was very hard for them to wake up. Everyone seemed to move in the slowest slow motion.

Hurry, hurry! I wanted to bark. *The day is ready to greet us!*

But I tried my best to be patient.
That can be very hard for a dog.
After everyone ate a good breakfast,
we were finally ready to go.

It was going to be a big day. The sheep's wool had grown too full, so Darnell needed me to help herd them so he could give the sheep haircuts. Actually, Darnell called it getting shorn, but the sheep liked to call it getting a haircut.

But there were other things we had to do before trimming the sheep.

We began the morning with our everyday farmyard chores. First, we fed Zonks and the other pigs. They were happy to see us, but even happier to see their trough filled with slop.

Then we brought feed to the horses.

Comet, the foal, said she was starving when we came. And I believed her! She took huge, gobbling bites of her breakfast.

Star and Grey were her parents. They were probably hungry too, but they were kind and let Comet eat first. When she was all done, Darnell chuckled and poured some more feed for Star and Grey.

Next we fed the cows and stopped by the chicken pen to toss seeds and kernels of corn.

Cheep cheep cheep, the chicks chirped as they scooted around the yard pecking at the seeds. You know, when those little chicks are hungry, they sure move fast.

At last we made it out to the field, where the sheep were scattered here and there.

"Bo, do you think you can herd these fluffy guys?" Darnell asked.

I barked *yes!*

"Good," he said. "Now go round up those sheep and bring them back to the barn. It's time to open the Baa Baa Shop!"

The Baa Baa Shop was what Darnell called the barn when he was shearing wool from the sheep. Wyatt and Imani thought it was a really funny name, but I didn't get the joke. Humans can be silly like that.

I bolted toward the sheep with Darnell's instructions in mind. It felt great to run through the field in the morning. There was just a little bit of dew left on the grass to cool off my belly. Plus, the sun began to pop up over the trees and warm my back. I was proud to be a good dog who could help out around the farm.

I ran to the first sheep and asked
him to head to the barn, because it
was time for a haircut. He nodded his
head and began to walk toward the
barn. I was off to a good start!

After gathering a few more sheep, I realized I hadn't seen Puffs. I stopped and  looked for a second, but I couldn't find him anywhere. Where could that little lamb have gotten to? Did he finally score a good hiding place?

I dashed around the field barking his name.

But as I ran, I noticed that some of the sheep I had sent to the Baa Baa Shop were not doing as I had asked.

So this time, I walked each of them over to the barn, one by one. But every few steps, they stopped to eat another bite of grass. They were moving so slowly. They dragged their feet. They forgot what they were doing.

A few of them even asked if I would carry them up to the barn because it was too far away and they were so hot from all their wool.

All I could do was roll my eyes. What was going on with these lazy sheep? Didn't any of them want to get a haircut?

Rock and Roll

After leading several sheep to the barn, I went looking for Puffs again. Hmm, sheep don't get great at hiding overnight, so where had he gone?

When I finally found him, I couldn't believe I hadn't spotted him sooner. He was standing on a rock at the far end of the field.

"Hey, Puffs," I said. "It's time to come down. Darnell is giving out haircuts."

But Puffs just shook his head playfully. He had a spark in his eye, and I could tell that he wanted to turn this rock into another one of his silly games.

"No!" he cried. "Not until you come up here and catch me, Bo!"

"I've got work to do, Puffs," I said. "Now's not a good time to play."

"You hear that, world?" Puffs yelled out. "Bo Davis is too scared to climb a little old rock!"

Now he'd done it. It was time to teach him a lesson. I put my front paws on the rock and tried to pull myself up, but I slipped. I tried it again using my claws to get a grip, but the cold, hard stone was too slick.

No one was happier about this than Puffs. He giggled and baaed with delight as I slipped and slid around the base of the rock.

"Stop laughing, Puffs," I said.

But he didn't. Instead, he called other sheep over to watch, and they started laughing at me too.

I looked at my paws. If they wouldn't work, I needed a new plan to get Puffs off that rock. I needed to try something different. So I barked really loudly. I mean, this bark was so loud that it echoed through the field. I hoped it would scare Puffs, but he didn't budge.

Next I tried swatting Puffs with my tail, but that didn't work either.

"Wow, Bo! You really can't do it, can you?" Puffs said. "Maybe we should start calling you No-Go-Bo!"

All the sheep watching gasped at Puffs's new nickname for me, and I felt an angry tingling in the back of my neck. Puffs had turned a silly game into something mean. And I do not like mean things.

As the young sheep laughed on top
of his rock, I backed up farther and
farther. Then I took a running start and
launched myself up onto that rock!
And it worked!

Actually, maybe it worked a little too well. I made it onto the rock, but I couldn't get my footing, so I slammed into Puffs. The two of us rolled off the rock and tumbled into the cool grass below.

My head was still spinning when
a very un-puffy sheep walked over.
The other sheep noticed him too and
wanted to know where he had gotten
his hair cut.

The shorn sheep explained that Darnell was giving trims at the Baa Baa Shop—which is exactly what I had been trying to tell everyone! I began to feel very frustrated.

Then Puffs and his friends headed to the barn without saying good-bye. Instead, they were all laughing about how No-Go-Bo couldn't even climb a silly rock.

Had Puffs finally found a game that I wasn't good at?

Nanny
Sheep

It's hard to not be good at something. As a puppy, I've always been lucky. There were so many things I was good at from the very first time I tried them.

Like escaping my gate! Wyatt and Imani love to tell me about my first night at home. I was supposed to stay in a gated area downstairs.

I liked it until everyone else went upstairs, and I was all alone.

Did I cry and whine about it? Well, maybe a little. But then I used my paws to open the gate and found the perfect place to go to sleep for the night. A cozy spot on the rug right between Wyatt's and Imani's bedrooms. Then I didn't feel lonely anymore.

And there were lots of other things
I was good at: racing, digging, playing
fetch, and tug-of-war.

But I wasn't very good at climbing rocks. Or herding sheep. And I'm supposed to be a sheepdog! At least, that's what Darnell told me. But herding was hard, especially with these stubborn sheep.

I rolled over in the grass and lowered my head. What was I doing wrong?

"Good morning, Bo," came a familiar and comforting voice. It was Nanny Sheep. She was standing on Puffs's rock looking down at me.

"Aww, even you can climb the rock." I whimpered. "What's wrong with me?"

Nanny Sheep hopped down off the rock and stood close to me.

"Bo, sheep have a very different kind of foot from what dogs have," she explained. "We have hooves, which make it easier for sheep to climb on uneven surfaces. You have paws, which can be good for climbing, but climbing rocks is not as easy as walking on the ground."

I smiled. "That makes me feel a little better. But it's not just rock climbing.

I really need to work on my herding skills. I feel like I'm letting Darnell down."

"I can help you with herding, Bo," Nanny Sheep offered. "Why don't you come back after lunch?"

Oh, that got my tail wagging like wild. Not only was Nanny Sheep going to teach me how to herd, but it was also lunchtime! I thanked her and ran back to the house, where a bowl of chow had my name on it.

5

I Think
I Can

After lunch I was in a pretty good mood again, but unfortunately that didn't last long.

Stretched out lazily on the porch were those darn barn cats, King and Diva.

I tried to sneak by them, but those cats were waiting for me.

"Aww, poor Bo," said Diva, with an unkind grin. "I heard the news. Did the great big puppy have trouble climbing the teeny tiny rock?"

I knew I shouldn't let them get to me, but I couldn't help it. I barked and barked, which set them running and brought Jennica out of the house.

"Are we going to play fetch?" I asked excitedly.

"No, Bo," said Nanny Sheep. "You are going to learn how to herd sheep."

I was confused. "Do I need a ball to herd sheep?"

That made Nanny Sheep laugh. "No, the ball will help you *learn* how to herd. I am going to kick the ball. You must chase it and nudge the ball with your nose to keep it moving toward the barn. If the ball rolls away from your path, you must give it a little push to make it go in the right direction."

"Quiet, Bo!" she scolded. "Those barn cats aren't bothering anyone, so you let them be!"

I hung my head low and stared at those mean cats as they slunk to the edge of the porch. Then I went on my way.

Luckily it was a beautiful day. The sun had slipped behind the clouds, and there was a light breeze that cooled the air.

Nanny Sheep was waiting for me by the rock.

"Oh no, are we climbing the rock again?" I asked, looking around. I definitely did not want an audience.

"No." Nanny Sheep nudged a red ball toward me with her nose. It was Wyatt and Imani's kickball.

I loved chasing that thing around. My tail started wagging at the sight of it.

"Quiet, Bo!" she scolded. "Those barn cats aren't bothering anyone, so you let them be!"

I hung my head low and stared at those mean cats as they slunk to the edge of the porch. Then I went on my way.

Luckily it was a beautiful day. The sun had slipped behind the clouds, and there was a light breeze that cooled the air.

Nanny Sheep was waiting for me by the rock.

"Oh no, are we climbing the rock again?" I asked, looking around. I definitely did not want an audience.

"No." Nanny Sheep nudged a red ball toward me with her nose. It was Wyatt and Imani's kickball.

I loved chasing that thing around. My tail started wagging at the sight of it.

"Are we going to play fetch?" I asked excitedly.

"No, Bo," said Nanny Sheep. "You are going to learn how to herd sheep."

I was confused. "Do I need a ball to herd sheep?"

That made Nanny Sheep laugh. "No, the ball will help you *learn* how to herd. I am going to kick the ball. You must chase it and nudge the ball with your nose to keep it moving toward the barn. If the ball rolls away from your path, you must give it a little push to make it go in the right direction."

"That seems easy enough," I said.

But it wasn't! First, Nanny Sheep kicked the ball away from the barn. I ran after it and gave it a nudge, but I did it too hard. The ball went flying in another direction away from the barn again.

After a few tries I started to get the hang of it. I wove from side to side, making sure the ball kept rolling in a nearly straight line until we reached the barn.

When I got there, Nanny Sheep was waiting.

"You took too long," she said. "Try it again. Guide the ball down to the rock and return here as fast as you can."

I ran back and forth with the ball over and over. At the end of each run Nanny Sheep would say one word: "Again."

So I ran again and again . . . and again.

Finally, after an hour, Nanny Sheep said, "Bo, I think you are ready to herd some real sheep now."

Fluffy
Flock

Junior was the biggest, fluffiest sheep of the flock.

He towered next to Nanny Sheep and looked down at me.

"Okay, Bo. Your mission is to guide Junior to the barn," Nanny Sheep told me.

"With the ball?" I asked.

She laughed. "Oh, silly pup. You're going to herd sheep instead of the ball this time!"

I leaned closer to Nanny Sheep and whispered, "But I don't know how, remember?"

"Yes, you do," she said. "You herd the sheep the same way you handled the ball. If Junior steps out of line, you guide him back into place."

I nodded, then looked at Junior. "Okay, let's go to the barn."

And just like that he walked . . . in the wrong direction. I darted to one side of him and nudged him back on track. To my amazement, it worked!

Until he stopped to eat some grass.
I nudged him again, but Junior kept
chomping away. With a sheep this big,
I figured there was only one way to get
his attention.

I barked my command this time.
"GET TO THE BARN NOW, MISTER!"

Now, I'm not a yeller, but that made
Junior march! He hiked all the way up
the hill and into the barn.

I ran back to Nanny Sheep and cheered. "I did it! I did it!"

Nanny Sheep smiled and said, "Now try herding two sheep."

So I did. Then all of a sudden, I was herding three, four, and five sheep!

When I was done, Nanny Sheep smiled at me and said, "Job well done, little pup!"

"Thanks for your help," I said. "I wish Puffs were here to see this. Where is he, anyway?"

Nanny Sheep looked around. "I'm sure he's off playing somewhere. That Puffs always has some kind of game hidden in his wool."

"You've got that right," I said as I turned to leave. "Thanks again!"

"It was my pleasure, Bo," she said.

Then I had a thought. "Hey, Nanny Sheep. I don't suppose you have any advice for how to handle two pesky barn cats, do you?"

Nanny Sheep shook her head. "Oh, there's no cure for those two cats."

That made me laugh because she was probably right!

As I was heading home, my friend Scrapper raced out of the woods to surprise me.

"Bo! Bo! Hey, Bo!" He yipped and sped over so fast that instead of stopping, he tumbled right past me.

"What's the rush?" I asked.

"Monster! I found a monster in the forest!" he barked excitedly. "Follow me!"

Well, what else was a pup to do? A monster in the forest? Now that was something I had to see for myself.

Monster
Hunt

The woods were a fun place to go—
even if you were searching for a
monster. I mean, just look at all the
squirrels to chase!

Plus, there were so many smells
to sniff. Plants, trees, and dirt, just to
start. There were plenty of animal
scents that I had never smelled too.

Maybe one of those smells belonged to Scrapper's monster, which he is always looking for!

This time Scrapper had spotted the
monster on a ledge near the river, so
we headed that way.

As I jogged beside him, I asked him what the monster looked like.

"It was big . . . but also little," said Scrapper. "And it was fluffy, and it climbed up the ledge really fast."

So, it was a big, little monster who could climb fast and was fluffy? This sounded very interesting.

"Did you talk to it?" I asked Scrapper.

He looked surprised. "No way, Bo! It's a monster! Monsters don't make friends. They make trouble."

I thought about that, and it made me feel a little bit sad. Even monsters deserve friends.

"Well, we don't know that *this* monster wants to make trouble," I explained. "We should try to say hello. That's what good neighbors do, after all."

We reached the river, and Scrapper pointed his nose toward the cliff next to a waterfall.

When I looked up, I actually saw something fluffy on the rocks, but it definitely wasn't a monster.

A Little
Help

"Puffs!" I shouted, because I knew that fluffy white hair anywhere.

Somehow that sneaky little sheep had wandered into the forest to climb up the rocky cliffside.

"This had better not be one of your silly games!" I called. "Come down and let's go home!"

But Puffs didn't move. He was frozen in place. I could tell from the look in his eyes that something was wrong. He was scared.

Then I realized what was going on. Puffs was stuck!

A few other young sheep stepped out from between the trees.

"Bo!" they said. "Thank goodness! We were playing hide-and-seek, and Puffs found the perfect hiding spot. But now he can't get down!"

Oh boy, I wanted to growl at the lambs, but I stayed calm.

"You all know that sheep aren't supposed to be in the forest ever," I reminded them.

"We know, Bo! And we're sorry!" they said. "If you get Puffs down, then we promise we'll never come back into the forest again!"

I studied the rock wall, wishing that Nanny Sheep could have given me climbing lessons as well as herding lessons.

The wall was steep, but I had to help Puffs. He was my friend. Plus, he was a sheep, and it was my job to keep the sheep safe. After all, I was a sheepdog!

I carefully pawed the rocks and took one slow step at a time.

When all four of my paws were balanced on the rocks, I stopped. The surface didn't feel right under the pads of my paws. The ground was too slippery and uneven. How in the world would I ever do this?

Suddenly I wasn't alone on the
rocks. Scrapper scrambled right
past me.

"Do you need some help, Bo?" he
asked.

I was very surprised to see him. "How did you do that?" I asked.

"Do what? Oh, you mean climb on the rocks?" he said. Scrapper quickly ran around in a little circle. "It's super easy if you know the secret!"

Boogie
Pup

Scrapper skipped down next to me like it was the easiest thing in the world. "The first step to climbing," he explained, "is to remember that walking on rocks is not like walking on the ground."

"Well, gosh, I already figured that out!" I said.

"Great! Then you're ready for the next step." Scrapper woofed. "The secret to climbing rocks is to make it fun and *not* scary."

I looked up at Puffs. He seemed a long way away. Nothing seemed fun or not scary about climbing up there.

"Umm, I don't really know how to do that," I told him.

"Well, I like to dance," Scrapper said.

"And how is that supposed to help me get to Puffs?" I asked.

Scrapper's tail wagged wildly. "Easy! Dancing makes me happy, so when I climb the rocks, I pretend I'm dancing over them. I mean, I don't go fast, but putting a little shimmy in my step helps me keep my balance."

I watched as Scrapper did a little jig over the rocks. I could see that the way his paws skipped over the rocks helped him keep his footing.

"Now you try," Scrapper called.

I *do* like to dance—not as much as I like running. But whenever I dance, I feel happy. So I gave a little shake of my tail and took a quick step forward. And another step and another, and soon I was hopping and bopping up the rocks.

Finally I reached Puffs, and the little sheep was so happy to see me, he baaed. "Wow, Bo, that was amazing! Is there anything you're not good at?"

"Well, I wasn't good at climbing rocks at first," I admitted. "But with good friends to help me, maybe anything is possible. Now let's get down . . . and I don't mean dance."

I taught Puffs how to *cha-cha-cha*
to the bottom of the rocks. We sang,
"One, two, cha-cha-cha," until we
reached solid ground.

Puffs hung his head as the other sheep flocked to him.

"Are you okay, Puffs?" I asked.

"Gee, Bo. I'm sorry for laughing at you earlier today," the young sheep apologized. "I would have been stuck there forever if you hadn't shown up. Can you ever forgive me?"

"Hey, it's okay, buddy," I said. "Now let's get you back to the farm before anyone notices you wandered off."

Herd You
Loud and Clear

Sheep are very smart creatures, but they're also very curious. This is why they need to be herded from place to place. And let me tell you, herding sheep through the woods is not easy!

Even with Puffs and Scrapper trying to help, I had to work hard to keep the other sheep together.

As we wound our way between the trees, one little sheep wandered off to check out a log. He licked it and made a funny face. I guess it didn't taste good. I bounded behind him and nudged him back to the other sheep.

Then a chipmunk skittered across the path. It startled two sheep at the front of the line. I guess they'd never seen a chipmunk before, because they started to follow it. I dashed after them and gave them a gentle push back to the flock.

We continued along until there was a loud tap-tap-tapping sound as a shower of acorns fell from an oak tree to the forest floor. The acorn attack made all of us jump—even me, although I knew it was just a squirrel up in the branches. Darn squirrels!

Scrapper ran up to me and said, "Hey, Bo, what if *that* was the monster?"

I woofed *no*, but the little sheep I was leading got scared once they heard the word "monster."

They scattered in all directions.

"Thanks, Scrapper," I huffed.

Then I ran back and forth, nudging one sheep after the other into one flock.

113

When we finally left the woods behind us and got back to the farm, Nanny Sheep was waiting for us. And she wasn't alone.

Comet was there with Star and Grey, Zonks, and a bunch of other sheep with very short haircuts.

Everyone cheered as I guided the sheep through the field.

"I knew you could do it, Bo," Nanny Sheep said with a big smile.

"Thanks, Nanny Sheep," I said. "It turns out that with some help from my friends, I can do a lot of things I didn't think I could."

"Speaking of which," said Scrapper, coming over, "do you think you can teach me to herd sheep too?"

"Sure!" I told him. "It starts with chasing one of these."

I nudged the red kickball toward Scrapper. And as he chased after it, I had a hunch he would make a great herding dog too.

Here's a peek at Bo's next big adventure!

GOOD D🐾G

Fireworks Night

You might not think that puppies are the kind of animals who are interested in secret forts, but guess what? We totally are!

This is Scrapper. He's my best dog friend. He lives one house over from the Davis farm.

An excerpt from *Fireworks Night*

There's a forest in between our homes, and we love to play there. But not today. Today we were playing at Scrapper's house.

Scrapper had three humans in his family. There's Tom and Rey and their son, Hank. Hank's a really great kid, but more importantly, he's an amazing ball-thrower.

Humans might not understand why dogs like to play fetch so much. But honestly, I can't see how it's so different from two people playing catch.

Only, fetch is better! You get to run all over the place and catch the ball—

An excerpt from *Fireworks Night*

or stick or Frisbee—in your mouth. Then you get to chew and slobber all over it!

What's not to love about that? Humans should try it sometime.

Plus, if it weren't for fetch, Scrapper and I would have never discovered *our* secret dog fort!

You see, we were playing a special game of fetch. Hank had a brand new bouncy ball. How bouncy was it? It was faster and bouncier than any ball I'd ever seen.

An excerpt from *Fireworks Night*